The Lady and the Christmas Brooch

Ruth A. Casie

The Lady and the Christmas Brooch

Timeless Scribes
Publishing

Timeless Scribes Publishing LLC

Print ISBN-13: 978-1-945679-99-5

Editor: The Editing Hall - Chris Hall
Cover Artist: Wicked Smart Designs - Darleen Dixon

Disclaimer: The Lady and the Christmas Brooch originally appeared in the anthology **Christmastide Kisses** published by The Bluestocking Belles, December 2023. This standalone edition has been revised and updated for your reading pleasure.

This edition published by arrangement with Timeless Scribes Publishing LLC.

www.TimelessScribes.com

Also by Ruth A. Casie

BARRINGTON'S BRIGADE
A Wraith at Midnight Anthology - My Heart's Song
A Marriage for the Marquess - Coming January 2025

♥ ♥ ♥

LYON'S DEN - Connected World
The Lyon's Gambit
The Lyon's Alliance
Night of Lyons Anthology - The Lady and the Lyon's Scandal

♥ ♥ ♥

THE LADIES OF SOMMER-BY-THE-SEA - Regency Romance
The Lady and Her Quill
The Lady and the Spy
The Lady and Her Duke
The Duke's Lost Love

RETURN TO THE LADIES OF SOMMER-BY-THE-SEA
The Lady and the Barrister
The Lady and the Earl
The Lady and the Rogue
The Lady and Her Secret

♥ ♥ ♥

THE STELTON LEGACY - Fantasy Romance
The Guardian's Witch
The Highlander's English Woman
The Maxwell Ghost

PIRATES OF BRITANNIA - Crossover Series - Pirate Romance
Donald (Sons of Sagamore)
Hugh (Sons of Sagamore)
Graham (Sons of Sagamore)
The Pirate's Jewel
The Pirate's Redemption

Also by Ruth A. Casie

♥ ♥ ♥

THE DRUID KNIGHT SERIES - Time Travel Romance
Knight of Runes
Knight of Rapture
The Red Slippers — A Short Story
The Druid Knight Tale I — A Short Story—Expanded
The Druid Knight Tale II — A Short Story
Timeless Keepsakes Vol 2 - The Druid Knight Tale III - **The Druid's Bond**

♥ ♥ ♥

Historical Romance Anthologies
The Spirit of Love Anthology - The Ghost of Whispering Hollows
Dragonblade Historical Recipe Cookbook
The Light of Love Anthology - The Lady and the Flame
Christmas Kisses Anthology - The Lady and the Christmas Brooch

♥ ♥ ♥

HAVENPORT SERIES - Contemporary Novellas
Happily Ever After
The Witching Hour
Never Say Never
Echoes of Betrayal
How to Marry a Stuart Brother
Heart of the Matter

♥ ♥ ♥

Prologue

October 1811
Sommer-by-the-Sea

Lady Genevieve Sinclair, daughter of the Duke and Duchess of Grenfell, trudged along Manor Road toward Grenfell Manor. She liked the raised road with a sharp slope on the right. It offered a clear view of the North Sea. Normally, this route provided her with an enjoyable walk, but not today. Today, fortune had abandoned her, and the weather gods were anything but kind.

She lifted her skirts and skillfully navigated the treacherous puddles that dotted the path. The relentless wind whipped at her, and the unyielding rain lashed out at her stinging her cheeks. She lowered her head and kept moving. What she wouldn't give for the warm weather of a St. Luke's Summer day right now.

As if that wasn't enough, a fierce gust of wind howled down the road, its force nearly toppling her. Her senses dulled amid the cacophony of waves crashing upon the shore and the torrential downpour. With no shelter nearby, she had no choice but to persist through the onslaught.

Her senses numb, she failed to see or hear the approaching horse and rider until they were almost on top of her. As the racing horse broke through the curtain of rain, she instinctively raised her hand over her head in a futile attempt to shield herself. The startled horse veered away. Its rider struggled to regain control. In the chaos, the horse reared. A startled cry escaped Genevieve's lips as she stepped back and stumbled on the rocks on the right side of the road.

Swift and sure, strong hands reached out and gripped her shoulders, pulling her to safety. Dazed, Genevieve gaze met the piercing silver-gray eyes of her rescuer and found a profound concern etched into his features.

Silent but determined, he guided her toward his horse.

"You'll catch your death in this downpour." He mounted the animal. "You can ride with me. Please give me your hand. I'll take you somewhere safe."

She shivered in her pelisse and hesitated, bewildered by the sudden turn of events. The day had started bright and sunny. How had she gotten into this predicament? The sailors at the town dock warned her against leaving, but she didn't listen. The day seemed perfectly fine.

"You're shivering," he noted, his voice deep and comforting. "Quickly now. You need to get dry and warm." With remarkable ease, he lifted her onto his lap, wrapping her inside the warmth of his coat.

"Where were you going?" he inquired, his voice a soothing rumble. Yet, it was not just his words that eased her mind, but the genuine warmth of his concern and sanctuary from the storm.

"Grenfell Manor," she managed to say through chattering teeth. A deep rumble resonated in his chest, and as she stole a glance at him, an unspoken understanding passed between them. In that moment, amidst the howling wind and relentless rain, a profound realization rushed through her body. She felt it in her bones, an undeniable and irreversible truth. The attraction between them had ignited with an intensity that matched the tempestuous weather.

Chapter One

14 November 1816
London

Genevieve glided down the stairs amidst the final flurry of her family moving into their London home on St. James Square for the holiday season.

"My lady," Mrs. McGuire, the housekeeper, greeted her in the foyer. "Her Grace asked that you see her in the morning room."

"Thank you, Mrs. McGuire."

Her mother's request was unusual. She preferred to spend her time directly after breakfast with Mrs. McGuire, overseeing house matters before visitors arrived. Actually, her mother was quite rigid with her schedule. There were moments when Genevieve imagined how her mother's adept and meticulous household management skills could seamlessly transfer into a valuable asset for Wellington and his army. Her mother already ran both the London and Sommer-by-the-Sea estates like a seasoned general.

Genevieve stifled a grin and made her way down the hall. In the distance, she saw her mother at the morning room table with the house accounts. She was elegant and composed, her auburn hair pulled back and perfectly styled. Her mother's hint of aloofness resulted from years of navigating her way through society.

Her mother followed the restrictive rules and expectations of society to the letter as well as repressive long-held traditions, all in the name of upholding the family's prestigious title. In her eyes, a person was only as good as their reputation.

Yet, beneath her mother's strict façade was a woman who loved her daughter deeply with a genuine concern for her well-being and future. Lady Grenfell took to heart that her primary responsibility was to ensure that her daughter was a proper lady with all the manners and education required. As with any mother of the *ton*, her ultimate goal was to secure a suitable marriage for her daughter and reinforce the family's position.

Much to her mother's chagrin, Genevieve had acquired many of her mother's traits, strong-willed and tenacious. So far, she refused to consider anyone her mother had suggested.

"You wanted to see me, Mother?" Genevieve pushed her thoughts aside and swept into the room.

Her mother lifted her head and smiled. "An invitation arrived for you in the morning's post." She handed Genevieve the envelope.

The seal on the outside had her heart pounding. She removed the invitation and read it, her excitement growing.

> *Dearest Lady Genevieve Sinclair,*
>
> *It is with great pleasure that we extend to you our most cordial invitation to partake in the merriments of a grand and enchanting Christmas ball hosted by His Grace, the Duke of Westerfield.*
>
> *The festivities shall commence on the eve of the 24th of December at 8 p.m. at His Grace's illustrious London home, Westerfield House, where the spirit of the holiday season shall weave its magic into every corner of the splendid halls.*
>
> *Prepare to be enthralled by a night of wondrous delights, including lively music, a delectable feast, and the company of distinguished guests from far and wide. As the chandeliers glisten above and the halls are adorned with holly garlands, we anticipate an evening filled with elegance, joy, and unbridled enchantment.*
>
> *Attire for the occasion shall be formal, adding to the splendor of the evening.*

In anticipation of your revered company, we remain,
His Grace, the Duke of Westerfield, and the esteemed
family of Westerfield House.

Genevieve lowered the card and placed it on the table, her mind swirling with thoughts about her mother's reaction. The Westerfield Christmas Ball was an annual event. The invitation was always addressed to the Grenfell family, yet Genevieve had never attended. Her mother deemed her too young, too impressionable, and too much of a Sinclair to attend, which translated into enjoying the evening much too much. Her mother tolerated the Westerfields, while her father thoroughly enjoyed their company.

The duke was a commanding figure. His steely gray eyes held a wealth of wisdom gathered from years of experience in the foreign office and palace. His appearance was deceptive. His ebony hair gracefully displayed the passage of time with streaks of silver-gray at his temples that made him look younger than his fifty-eight years.

"I'm surprised you received your own invitation." Her mother went back to her work. "Well, you'll simply have to—"

"Graciously accept," her father's voice echoed, drawing their attention as he entered the room. "It's time Genevieve knew the Westerfields more than just in passing. Westerfield is my partner in several ventures. He is not the monster you make him out to be." He came up behind Genevieve. "Besides," he said to her, "His Grace is quite charming."

Her father exuded a congeniality and compassion that stood in stark contrast to her mother's demeanor. His personality possessed an amiable charm and a warmth that endeared him to others and set him apart from his contemporaries. His graying hair framed a face that exuded a gentle, reassuring presence, and his brown eyes held a glimmer of understanding that could soothe even the deepest troubles. To Genevieve, he was a fountain of knowledge and comfort during the stormiest of times.

Unlike her mother, he embraced a more open-minded perspective, valuing not just the social graces but also Genevieve's spirited curiosity. He encouraged her to seek knowledge and understanding that extended far beyond the confines of societal expectations, nurturing her inquisitive nature and fostering a deep bond between them.

Regrettably, her father was often caught in the struggle between her mother's traditional views and his desire to see Genevieve happy. She thought him a good ship's captain, guiding her through a tempest named Beatrice.

"Charles, surely you're not serious. Why Genevieve is—"

"To be twenty-one on Christmas day." Her father gave her his full attention. "I think a special gown is in order for the occasion." He turned to his wife. "You wouldn't want the Westerfields to think poorly of us or, worse, that we hold them responsible for something that happened almost a hundred years ago. Would you?"

Genevieve was shocked into silence. Her father was playful, but still, she had never seen her parents at odds, at least not when she was present.

Her mother looked down at the invitation. "Genevieve, you've always found a reason to decline. Do you want to go?"

Genevieve glanced at her father. He gave her a slight nod of encouragement.

She turned to her mother. "I've declined because I'm usually not in London at Christmas. I've stayed at Sommer-by-the-Sea. I would like to attend."

Genevieve sensed an unspoken tension building in her mother, like an approaching storm on the horizon. As her mother's gaze shifted between her and her father, Genevieve couldn't ignore the growing intensity that hinted at a turning point.

"You'll be twenty-one on Christmas Day. While your father and I have allowed you a great deal of freedom and independence, it's time to consider suitors seriously." Her mother's eyes softened as she directed her gaze directly at her. "Genevieve, it's crucial that we reach a decision together by Christmas."

A sobering realization settled over Genevieve as her mother went on, her words filled with both love and gentle rebuke. "If you do not choose a suitor"—her mother let out a long sigh—"you will leave us with no alternative but to select one for you. Westerfield's Christmas ball is spectacular." Her mother lifted her head, her features unreadable, leaving Genevieve with the understanding that the course of her future had just been set.

Chapter Two

The Grenfell carriage rolled to a stop before the grand Westerfield House. Genevieve's father, the first to disembark, braved the brisk weather with the clear evening sky and a subtle hint of snow in the air. He assisted his wife and daughter out of the carriage. Genevieve and her mother quickly smoothed their gowns before being escorted to the entrance.

Genevieve's smile broadened as they stepped into the entrance. A footman relieved her of her new green bombazine cloak, elegantly trimmed with white fox. She glanced around, absorbing the hall's grandeur while waiting for her parents, and then together, they made their way to the receiving line.

As she followed her parents into the foyer, she was unable to resist studying every detail. The floorplan with the white marble foyer and adjoining rooms was similar to Grenfell House, a familiar yet novel sight. She took a deep breath and enjoyed the aroma of cinnamon and apples. Swags of pine and holly garlands dressed every corner, lending a touch of warmth and softening the austere rooms. The enchanting atmosphere added to Genevieve's expectations for the evening ahead.

The receiving line moved steadily. Genevieve's excitement grew until, finally, it was their turn. Filled with anticipation, she and her parents approached their host.

"Westerfield, you know my wife, the Duchess of Grenfell." Her father gestured toward her mother.

"Of course I do." Westerfield gave her father a gracious nod and turned his attention to her mother. "It has been some time since we were last together, Your Grace. I hope you and all your family will honor us with your presence more often."

"Thank you, Your Grace." Her mother paused for a heartbeat. Gradually, her tone softened as the barriers—often erected and stood behind when with the *ton*—began to fade. "We *should* be together more often. I don't believe you've had the pleasure of seeing our Genevieve recently." Her mother stepped to the side.

Positioned slightly behind her parents, Genevieve stepped forward. "Your Grace, thank you for including me in this evening's festivities."

The Duke of Westerfield leaned closer and whispered in her ear, "That is much too formal for family."

Shocked, her eyes widened, and she turned to him in surprise. "Family?" She glanced at her uneasy mother. "I had no idea."

"Warren, really." Her mother's smile twinkled as Genevieve had never seen. "The relationship has never been confirmed. You know that as well as I do."

Westerfield's lips turned up in a sly mischievous expression, and he once again gave his attention to Genevieve. "The evidence is there. I think you will have to prove it to her, though. She doesn't want to listen to me."

Lady Grenfell chuckled. "Are you going to tell her the same story you told me all those years ago?"

"What story?" Genevieve fixed her gaze on her mother, who appeared uneasy despite her usual strong, stalwart manner.

Her mother glanced at Westerfield, the invisible barrier returning. "You'll forgive me, Your Grace. I wouldn't want to take up more of your time." Her mother placed her hand on her father's arm, ushering him forward.

Confused by her mother's behavior, Genevieve watched them walk away. "What is she hiding?" she wondered aloud.

"It's not what she's hiding." Westerfield's expression grew serious. "It's not something that happened, but more about something lost for over a century. Some view my fascination with the situation as a mere yearly amusement. Yet, I assure you that it holds a profound significance. The elusive Christmas brooch has yet to be found.

"Some, like your mother, do not believe the brooch exists. Some people do not have a heart deep enough to find it. One must abandon logic and what you know in order to locate it. But that is not where the quest ends. You must decipher its message." Westerfield studied Genevieve.

"To do that, a new perspective is needed. I have a very good feeling about tonight. Your mother once tried to find the treasure, but she did not succeed." Westerfield spoke, glancing at Lady Grenfell, who was staring back at him, holding Genevieve's dance card. He brought his attention back to Genevieve. "Are you ready to find the key to your destiny? Not everyone is willing."

"My destiny? But how, Your Grace?" Genevieve asked, intrigued by the mysterious proposition, Westerfield held her full attention. Her destiny? This was far beyond having her tea leaves read by Tatiana when she went to the woman's tearoom in Sommer-by-the-Sea.

"Find the brooch," he urged, scanning the room. "It is somewhere here in the house. The brooch shall reveal the secrets of your destiny. You have until the last stroke of midnight to find it."

"And what happens after midnight?"

"Why, it's Christmas Day. You'll have to wait an entire year to try again. I hope you will take up the challenge. You see, it was one hundred years ago today that the brooch was lost."

"I've always enjoyed a challenge." She could keep busy and avoid her mother and the ballroom. Genevieve nodded and turned to leave but halted midstep.

"Have you changed your mind already?" he teased with a playful smirk. Genevieve glanced over her shoulder, catching sight of his devilish smile. It made her step back in front of him. For a moment, she found herself captivated by his charm. Her breath caught as a flush ran up her neck, leaving her cheeks tinged with color. His Grace's knowing gaze revealed he was fully aware of her thoughts.

"Not at all." She refused to acknowledge the fast tattoo of her pounding heart. "I have one question, Your Grace. Will finding my destiny harm anyone?"

Westerfield gazed at her without answering immediately. "How can finding the key to your destiny do any harm? It's possible that following your destiny could upset some people." He studied her closely as he spoke. His playful smile turned into a more admiring expression than a roguish one. "In all the years I've waited for someone to find the brooch, only one other person has ever asked that question."

Genevieve took a breath, eager to know more. "Who—"

"No," he interrupted firmly, a roguish glint in his eye. "I shall not tell you. That is, not until you've successfully found the brooch."

"My curiosity has me eager to find out who you're protecting. I suppose I shall have to deliver the brooch to you before midnight." Genevieve's excitement grew at the prospect of the challenge. "I hope I don't disappoint you."

"I don't think you could ever disappoint anyone," His Grace assured her, turning up his charm.

"You never asked about the rules," he pointed out.

"I learned a long time ago that seeking forgiveness is preferable to seeking permission. I am certain that, if there were rules that needed to be followed, you would have informed me. That said, I would like to know if you have any suggestions. Where should I begin?"

"There are several people attending this evening who can assist you. There are others who… well, let me say their advice would be best ignored. That is all I shall say. Enjoy the festivities and the hunt. Make sure to see the library. There used to be a family tree on the library wall, but someone removed it before you were a gleam in your mother's eye. See if you can find it. Now off with you before your mother sends Wellington to save you."

Genevieve gracefully glided toward the ballroom. Her desire to uncover the key to her destiny surpassed her eagerness to unravel the brooch's mysteries.

Chapter Three

Having had enough of the evening's Christmas festivities, Alexander, Viscount Ashford, the notorious rake, nursed a mild headache from the afternoon's celebration with his friends. He couldn't fathom why he had promised his uncle, Westerfield, he'd attend his annual affair. In the past, Ashford had carefully planned to be conveniently away from London on Christmas Eve, avoiding the family event.

Yet, a promise was a promise, and so he quickly found himself surrounded by eager mothers with marriageable daughters as well as widows seeking a provider. However, those women hinted at a liaison rather than a life-long commitment.

Now, at his uncle's suggestion, he and his aching head sought refuge in the library, confident no one would ever discover him here. With the fire crackling, he lay on the comfortable leather sofa with his eyes closed and tried to relax, hoping the throbbing ache in his head would soon subside.

The soft click of the latch alerted him that someone entered the room, their footsteps silent as a whisper. By God's blood, was some mother trying to corner him, or worse, was some secret rendezvous taking place? Before he could reveal his presence, a flash of red silk skirts brushed past him and stood at the bookshelves in front of him.

From his vantage point, he studied the woman intently, convinced she had no clue that the room was occupied. Her figure was slender, her glossy black hair coiled in a low chignon resting on the nape of her neck. God's blood, he hadn't lost enough in gambling the previous night. Now, he found he was wagering against himself, pondering the color of her eyes. Tawny brown? No, he thought not.

Cerulean blue? Perhaps, he nodded to himself. But no, they had to be an emerald green.

The woman retrieved a book from the shelf and stepped back, engrossed in the text. She took another step farther back. Despite knowing he should speak up, he was stunned into silence.

Another step and the back of her legs were against the sofa. Still, he remained silent, captivated by the imminent collision. She settled into the seat, quickly turned, and dropped the book onto the floor. Startled, she couldn't find the words or actions to respond. She simply stared at him in surprise.

♥ ♥ ♥

Genevieve's gaze locked with a man whose piercing silver gray eyes held a hint of mystery. Those eyes had admired her before, but she struggled to recall where until he smiled. Westerfield. He looked just as she had imagined Westerfield would look if he were twenty-five years younger.

What unsettled her even more was the instant connection she felt, leaving her unsure what to do or say.

"I would help you up, Lady Genevieve, but you are sitting on top of me." His remark was casual as he glanced at their position.

She looked down at where she was perched but remained motionless, unable to find her voice.

"I shall tell you that I am used to beautiful women being on top of me, but usually, we are without any hindering clothes," he added teasingly.

Genevieve's eyes widened at his bold remark, and to her surprise, she did the strangest thing—she laughed heartily. When she looked back at him, his dismissive glance had transformed into a warm, playful smile setting off a spark of familiarity between them.

"At least I have put you in your place, my lord." Genevieve's gaze shifted from the sofa to his charismatic eyes. "But you have me at a disadvantage. Have we been introduced?" She peered over the back of the sofa before focusing on him. "I could call for His Grace. I am sure he would accommodate us."

With as much grace as she could muster, Genevieve rose from her seat on top of him, forgetting the book on the floor, and stepped a few paces away.

"That won't be necessary. I regret I have not made a better impression on you, although you were a young girl the last time we spoke." He replaced his teasing tone with a sincere manner as he gazed at her.

Startled by his words, Genevieve tried to recall who he was. Surely, she would remember a handsome, charming man like him.

"I believe we were in Sommer-by-the-Sea, and you were fifteen years old. Your mother was quite adamant that I leave."

Inwardly, Genevieve cringed as memories of that afternoon resurfaced. She had often revisited the event in her mind, giving it alternative endings. A gallant young man finds her caught in an unexpected downpour while she traipses through the cold October rain on her way home from the village. The relentless rain blocks her vision, and she fails to see or hear the approaching horse and rider until they were almost on top of her. The horse shies away as she steps back dangerously close to the steep incline. The rider, genuinely concerned for her well-being, delivers her home, where her mother is grateful for her safe return and honors the man. Alone with him for a brief moment, in gratitude, she kisses her savior.

"Lord Ashford," she exclaimed, the spark of recognition rushing to her brain. "I didn't recognize you, dry. The rain did you well." Her gaze traveled from the toes of his boots all the way up his tall, handsome frame. "You've grown into quite the striking man."

"Oh, my dear Lady Genevieve, you have blossomed into a beautiful flower." His gaze was appreciative but not leering. "I knew when you turned and faced me that I would see emerald-green eyes. It's an eye color for which I have a particular fondness. I'm glad you recovered.

"But we best leave. The *ton* won't stand for us being alone together, least of all you with me. I wouldn't want to incur your mother's wrath again." He shook his head and glanced at the floor as if reliving the embarrassment.

"I am more than willing to share with anyone who inquires that I found you lost, wandering in the hall." His tone was tinged with a hint of disappointment.

A numb, empty feeling washed over her as if a bucket of cold water had doused her. Genevieve's spine straightened as the memory of her mother's embarrassing actions rushed back.

"How dare you accept a ride from a stranger." The young soldier came to her rescue again. He reminded her mother that he could have left her to die on the road instead of ensuring her safe return home. The fact that Lord Ashford still remembered the incident was humiliating.

"Thank you for your very gallant offer. You can stay if you like.

I want to look for something while I'm here in the library. But please, if you decide to go, close the door quietly when you leave." Heat ran up her neck, staining not only her cheek but her temper. It was best if he left, especially considering her mother's potential wrath. Ashford might have dealt with many things in his life, but he had yet to see her mother's full fury.

Besides, his reputation preceded him. Lord Ashford was a rogue of the worst order. A charming problem whose presence would undoubtedly fuel the gossip mills and draw unwanted attention to her and her respectable family.

She took the fallen book from the floor, retrieved a folio from the bookcase, and settled at the large table. He hadn't moved. Browsing through the book's parchment leaves, she was determined to focus on her work and dismiss any thoughts of his presence in the room. He still hadn't moved.

♥ ♥ ♥

Ashford arched an eyebrow, surprised by Genevieve's sudden change of heart. "Well, if you're sure," he said, a hint of amusement in his voice, and walked closer to the table. "I wouldn't want to be a distraction. I'll be quiet as a mouse while you work, although I do find that strange since you are attending a ball. Should you need help, however, I'm quite familiar with the library and its contents. What are you looking for?"

Genevieve lifted her head. "The location of the Christmas brooch."

Ashford's curiosity was piqued, and he put his hand over what Genevieve was reading. "On whose invitation are you looking for the Christmas brooch?"

She lifted her chin and stared at him for several heartbeats before a smile tilted the corners of her mouth. She pulled out the chair next to her.

"I would venture to say, the same person who charged you with being in the library. Westerfield." She glanced at the mantel clock. "Have a seat so we can begin. There are fewer than three and one-half hours left until midnight."

"Does that mean you're declaring a truce?" Ashford asked, a hopeful glimmer in his eyes as he sat beside her.

"Yes," Genevieve replied, meeting his gaze with newfound sincerity.

"We should seal our pact." With a gentle intensity, he leaned closer and kissed her lips.

Surprised by the suddenness of his kiss, she was momentarily speechless. As he deepened the kiss, her mind questioned whether his affection was genuine or simply the behavior of a charming rogue. Yet as his hand reached out, pulling her nearer, her thoughts dissolved into the enchantment of the moment.

When he finally drew back, the lingering memory of his kiss, the warmth of his lips remained. As their gazes locked, a flicker of vulnerability danced in his eyes. In that charged instant, an unspoken understanding, as delicate as a whisper yet as powerful as a promise, filled the space between them.

Barriers each of them had built around their hearts fractured and crumbled, replaced by a sense of empathy and mutual recognition. The profound shift not only bridged the gap between their souls but also laid the foundation for an unbreakable connection, an undeniable bond that shimmered with the potential of something extraordinary yet to unfold.

Chapter Four

"I'm glad you didn't want to seal our pact in blood." A sweet smile graced Genevieve's lips. She noticed Ashford blinking, more than slightly surprised by her quick wit, and thoroughly enjoyed being on the receiving end of it. Westerfield's challenge was quickly becoming more intriguing.

"I noticed several folios filled with the family history. We could start there." She didn't wait for his answer. In truth, she needed some distance. Not too far. But distance just the same. She was aware of Ashford's reputation, and while she felt more alive than she ever had before, she wasn't reckless.

They worked quietly together, searching through the folios.

"Why did you accept Westerfield's challenge?" Ashford sat surrounded by several books and leafed through the pages as he waited for her answer.

"Like you, I do not care for events like this. I find the constant scrutiny and expectations from the *ton* suffocating. I must watch who I speak with. Am I laughing too loud? Have I unintentionally offended someone?" She put down the pencil and rested her clasped hands on the parchment in front of her. "I am a tool for my family as you are for yours. This challenge is a welcome adventure. I've found I always learn something when I veer off the path I'm expected to take. And this, my friend, is as far from my path as I have ever been."

"We are kindred spirits in that way. I can now see why Westerfield plotted for our paths to cross. He wanted us to work together."

"Plotted? What do you mean?" Genevieve tilted her head, her

brows drawn together. She smiled inwardly, realizing that this interaction with Ashford was becoming more captivating by the moment.

"Westerfield told me I'd find something in the library that would clear my headache."

Genevieve gasped. "He suggested I begin my search in the library."

"So, he both plotted and manipulated us into this situation. I thought his request was unusual, especially during his Christmas Ball." Ashford chuckled. "I can see his satisfied smug smile. He wanted us together. His delight when I arrived this evening caught me off guard, and how he rubbed his hands together gave off an air of scheming. In retrospect, it's logical to assume he was eager for us to collaborate in the quest for the Christmas brooch. Would you agree?"

"I don't like being manipulated. Westerfield could have asked."

He understood her annoyance. He had years of experience with Westerfield. His uncle's skills had been developed in Parliament, where lives were at stake, and negotiation and even manipulation were fair game.

"Westerfield's maternal grandmother, Isabella, the Duchess of Douglaston, was in her seventies when she told Westerfield the story about the lost Christmas brooch. Ever since then, he's tried to find the brooch. Despite his father dismissing it as an old woman's ranting, his mother believed in the tale. She encouraged her son never to give up," Ashford explained.

"Do you believe there is a brooch?" Genevieve asked.

Her eyes, her beautiful green eyes, searched his for any hint of agreement.

"One that is the key to your destiny?"

Ashford, captivated by her intense gaze, contemplated the possibilities she suggested. Could their destinies indeed be intertwined? He had thought so five years ago. He convinced himself their brief encounter was just that. But her emerald eyes had haunted him. He turned away from her gaze to break the spell.

For the moment, it didn't matter what he thought. Genevieve believed in the story, and that was all that mattered. The enchantment of her world and the spark of a promised destiny surrounded them. Perhaps it was Christmas magic, but he would move heaven and earth to find the Christmas brooch if it existed, and know his destiny.

"At this moment, I do believe the brooch exists. I have never known my uncle to lead me astray."

The mantel clock struck the half-hour and interrupted their conversation. He glanced at the timepiece. "Half past eight. We best keep searching. Midnight shall arrive sooner than we think."

"We searched the three folios that were conveniently labeled 'Christmas Brooch' but found little information." Genevieve closed one of the folios and scanned the bookshelves.

"They contain the accounting of previous searches without any clear evidence." He began to return the papers to the folio. "We should be looking at journals and estate receipts prior to the 24th of December 1716."

"Why that date?"

Ashford paused before he responded. "I would have thought Westerfield had told you. A great tragedy involving the Christmas brooch happened in the house on the 24th of December 1716. It's the reason he has his annual Christmas ball and challenge."

He took the folio from her and returned it to its designated place.

"The library is organized into four major sections: History, Philosophy, Fine Arts, and Westerfield House." Ashford helped her from her seat and guided her along the bookcase toward the back of the room. "Each category is further divided. For example, the Westerfield House section is divided by the tenure of each duke."

They stopped when they found the section labeled *Westerfield House* and began examining the lower shelves.

"The older books are on the top shelves." He moved in front of her and began to identify the books crammed into the shelves while Genevieve examined the lower shelves.

"Westerfield's maternal great grandfather, Thomas Talbot, was awarded the Duchy of Douglaston in 1676. His son, Henry, succeeded him in 1717." Ashford explained, pointing to older journals on the top shelves. "These are not as well organized as I had hoped. It could take hours to find the correct journal and estate files."

Genevieve struggled to retrieve a journal from the shelf, but it was caught by another one crammed on top of it.

"Here, let me help you," Ashford offered, working the journal back and forth until he got a better grip on the diary and pulled it free. He blew off the dust and handed it to Genevieve.

As she fanned the discolored pages, a letter that had been tucked among the pages fell to the floor.

Ashford knelt and retrieved the document, handling it delicately. As he unfolded the aged parchment, his eyes fell upon the elegant cursive writing skillfully penned by an expert hand.

"What does it say?" Genevieve peered over his shoulder and tried to read the faded ink.

"My Dearest."

Ashford's voice was mellow, his tone reverent.

"As I pen these words, I am filled with emotions too vast to contain. I write to you from the depths of my heart, hoping that one day these words shall find their way to you and, with them, the profound love I have for you."

How odd. There was a comfort in the cadence of the sentences. Ashford read words he could easily have written. His voice softened, and he continued,

"We find ourselves living in a world that seeks to separate us with its rigid conventions and expectations. But within society's boundaries, my heart has found its freedom with you. Your spirit, your wit, and your beauty have enthralled me beyond measure, and I find myself unable to resist you.

"In the grand halls of this house, where we first exchanged glances, I knew that fate had bound us together at that very moment. Like the colors of a vibrant painting, our hearts are intertwined, forming a bond that surpasses time and defies the restrictions of our station.

"My dearest Camille,"

Genevieve's breath hitched as she inhaled deeply.

"Should I stop?" Ashford asked, lowering the document, worried that the love letter might have offended her.

"No, please. Continue," Genevieve insisted, her voice a whisper.

As Ashford stared at her, stirred by curiosity, he was certain something in the letter startled her. He raised the parchment once more and continued to read on, eager to discover the truth. He and Genevieve shared an unspoken understanding, a mutual passion for unearthing the secrets of the past that united them on this journey.

"I implore you to follow your heart as I follow mine. Let not the rules of society dictate our fate, for true love can surmount any obstacle."

The words on the page moved something inside him. A glance and he saw it in Genevieve's face as well. This letter applied to them as well as to Camille and her lover.

"With each passing moment, my desire to be with you grows stronger, and I long for the day when we can openly express our affection without fear or reservation.

"As I place my hopes within these words to you, I dream of a future where we can be united without any restrictions, where the brooch that bears our devotion shall frame our adoration for each other like an exquisite work of art. Our love thrives and blossoms in this house's hidden corners and halls. I pray that one day, we shall find the courage to break free from the chains that bind us.

"Until that day comes, know that my heart remains forever devoted to you. No distance or circumstance shall weaken the love I hold for you, my dearest Camille, my flower, my beauty,

"All my love is yours.

"Loren"

He handed her the letter. "Can I assume your middle name is Camille?"

She lifted her head quickly. "Yes. How did you know?"

"Your gasp when I read it out loud." He gazed at her and fought to keep the moment's magic, but he couldn't keep reality away. "I wonder if this is some sort of jest from Westerfield."

Genevieve took the letter from him and examined it carefully. "I do not think this is a deception."

He gazed in surprise as she rubbed the paper between her fingers.

"It's possible the paper is a hundred years old." Then she ran her fingers lightly over the back of the paper. "I don't sense any indentation from a writing implement other than the words you read." She turned the paper right side up. "Nor is there any indication that the original ink has been scraped off and the paper reused." She handed the document back to him. "No. I think the letter and the message are real. It is beautifully written and penned."

Ashford stared at her with newfound admiration. Her attention to detail and logical deductions were impressive. "So, Loren was a man who lived here a century ago, and he wrote this letter to Camille."

Genevieve nodded. "It seems that way. But who were they? And how can their Christmas brooch have any impact on our destiny?"

"We shall find out," Ashford said with determination, "before the clock strikes midnight. I must admit, I had my doubts we'd find anything. Not because I doubted we'd find a clue," he quickly added, "but because there were so many places to search."

"I am fortunate to have noticed the journal squeezed into the small space. Although, I shall admit the journal underneath it was my goal. It's a coincidence." She cast a fleeting glance at him over her shoulder and noticed the clock on the desk. "It's nearly ten o'clock. We only have two hours."

Ashford drank in Genevieve's lingering gaze, recognizing the longing in her eyes as a silent plea for comfort and closeness. Perhaps it was the enchantment the letter had cast over them.

He drew her into his embrace, cradling her tenderly, her head nestled under his chin while her arms wound around his waist. They held each other. Her heart beating in harmony, a strong, steady rhythm reflecting the resilient emotional bond and closeness between them.

"It could even be destiny," he murmured. Both of them silently acknowledged the possibility that something beyond Westerfield, even beyond chance, may have brought them together.

Chapter Five

The brooch must exist. The words echoed in Ashford's head as he gently rubbed Genevieve's back, comforted with her in his arms. How had she managed to rekindle feelings that had lain dormant for five years?

With Lady Grenfell working against him at their first encounter, he knew courting Genevieve was out of the question. Even he had to admit she had good reasons. A third son without any prospect of land or funds, and whose only reputation was that of the *ton's* most recent rogue, were different from the credentials that would endear him to any mother.

"Come in front of the fire before you catch your death. What were you doing out in this weather? I would think you were cozy and warm at the inn." Ashford *followed his uncle into the library and stood before the fire. "Why the scowl, or should I ask who you antagonized?"*

"On my way here, I came upon Lady Genevieve making her way to Grenfell Manor."

His uncle turned his head toward him, his eyebrow lifted.

"I brought her to her parents. Lady Grenfell gave me a piece of her mind."

"Ah, the over-protective mother hen. You played the gallant knight."

Ashford swung around. "Did you expect me to let the poor girl drown, fall down that steep incline, or worse, get run over by a carriage? I almost ran her down. The rain was coming down in sheets, and all Lady Grenfell cared about was that we had not been properly introduced, and my attention toward her daughter would not be tolerated."

His anger subsided as confusion took its place. "I tucked the young woman inside my coat to keep her warm." A man of quick wit, he struggled to find the correct words to explain what was inside of him. "Mine... I know that sounds strange, but she's mine."

Westerfield stared at him for several heartbeats. "Then why are you here?"

Ashford looked at his uncle and studied his mentor. "Because Lady Grenfell was correct. I have nothing to offer Lady Genevieve. I am... not the type of man her daughter deserves."

"What do you plan to do about it?"

Ashford warmed his hands in front of the fire. "Accept your offer to buy me a commission in Wellington's service."

"Running away, are we?" His uncle chuckled as he stood at the cellarette and poured himself a whisky. The man's attitude and glib remark raised Ashford's temper.

He quickly quieted his response. He had given his uncle—and others—every reason to believe he was an irresponsible rogue. He saw that now.

"Not at all. I'm running to become the person you always told me I was meant to be."

His uncle's back straightened. He turned and faced him with a smile that indicated he was pleased and proud. "You won't regret it." Westerfield handed him a whisky. "To your success."

He went off to war, dreaming of hair as black as coal and eyes the color of fine emeralds.

Now she was in his arms.

"Where should we begin?" They relaxed their grip on each other. Genevieve raised the letter and showed Ashford.

"Loren mentions flowers and paintings. Perhaps the conservatory?" Genevieve looked up at Ashford. "Westerfield does have a conservatory, doesn't he?"

Ashford stepped away and ran his hand through his hair. "No, not really. There is a greenhouse across the garden. Let me see the letter."

He took the letter from Genevieve. "Here"—he pointed to the letter—"it clearly says, *in the hidden corners of the house.* I don't think we'll find anything in the greenhouse."

"Perhaps the staff has a special room where they work with the plants for decorating the house."

"We can ask Benson." Ashford had some hope.

He tucked the letter into his doublet and gave her his arm. "My lady, I'm certain Benson will guide us to the right place."

She gave him a breathtaking smile and looped her arm in his. "Most definitely, my lord. You lead the way. I have no idea where we are going."

Ashford bent down, his lips close to her ear. "My lady, that is a very dangerous thing to say. How do you know I won't take you somewhere where no one will hear you should you need assistance?" He led her to the door.

"I can only hope." Genevieve blinked her eyelashes and smiled.

Ashford stopped in his tracks, his eyes twinkling, his smile warm and inviting. He took her in his arms and kissed her deeply.

She didn't resist but instead drew him closer.

Somewhere a clock struck the hour. They both hesitated and counted off the chimes. Eight. Nine, Ten.

"Our choice, my lady. Continue this lovely rendezvous or search for the brooch. I shall be most honest. Nothing would please me more than to bruise your lips and feel your body. But we made a pact with Westerfield, and no one has come this close."

"If the prize should elude us…" She looked deeply into his eyes. "I shall still be here."

He kissed her nose. "As shall I. Come, my adventurer, to Benson. We shall take the short way through the gallery of old dukes. We may even be able to find the illustrious Thomas Westerfield and his wife, Mary. I am assuming that the Loren in the letter is the brother of the Duchess."

With her arm laced through his, they navigated the hidden passages of Westerfield House. The anticipation and thrill of adventure excited her, and she knew it did Ashford as well. In this night of secrets and revelations, Genevieve was one with Ashford and their shared purpose, seeking a treasure and the possibility of a love that had withstood the test of time.

The echoes of their soft laughter and whispers filled the ancient halls as they willingly ventured into the mysteries of their intertwined destinies.

Ashford led her through a door and closed it behind them. A long hall stretched out in front of them, adorned with formal portraits of each Westerfield duke.

"This hallway leads from the breakfast room to the other side of the house. We haven't the time to pay our respects to each duke, but we should be able to say hello to Thomas. The portraits should be in chronological order. Thomas's tenure began in 1676."

They went down the hall, reading brass plaques and glancing at solemn portraits.

"Ah, here it is." They both looked at the man. "He appears very strict and somewhat unhappy."

Genevieve glanced at the picture next to it. "This picture seems out of place for a portrait gallery."

Ashford joined her in front of an intricately painted and enticing garden scene. Four people were in the garden looking at the sky. "You're right. This doesn't belong here, although it is a casual portrait of Thomas and Mary with two young boys."

"Their sons?"

"They only had one child. The bigger boy is their son Henry. The other boy is young Loren, Mary's brother."

"This must be the garden Loren mentioned in his letter." Genevieve studied the picture. "Do you have any idea what the next clue could be?"

Ashford shook his head. "No, I don't. It won't be something obvious."

Ashford pulled the letter out of his doublet and reread it. Moments later, Ashford's eyes widened, his astonishment clear. "God's blood. It's right here," he muttered.

Genevieve peered over his shoulder. "Where?"

I dream of a future where we can be united without any restrictions, where the brooch that bears our devotion shall frame our adoration for each other like an exquisite work of art. Our passion thrives and blossoms in the house's hidden corners and halls.

"The significant words are frame, hall, and blossoms. It all fits." He gave the letter to Genevieve and carefully ran his fingers around the frame.

"I don't think you'll find anything there. The staff could easily come upon it. No. It has to be concealed. Perhaps on the back."

Ashford removed the picture from the wall. They both inspected the back. Nothing.

Disappointed, Ashford lifted it to replace it on the wall.

"Wait." Genevieve stayed his arm. She removed a hairpin from her chignon and placed it in a slit in the frame. In the stillness of the hall, they both heard a soft click and immediately looked at each other.

"See if you can pry out the piece of wood. I'll hold the frame."

With care, Genevieve worked her hairpin in the slot and successfully revealed the hidden compartment. Inside, she found a small, rolled-up parchment aged by time.

Ashford placed the frame on the floor as Genevieve read the scroll.

> "In halls of grandeur, where art meets time,
> A love once bloomed, a hidden climb.
> Behind this frame, a secret lies,
> To find the brooch, follow these lines.
> A painting's brush, a lover's heart,
> A bond that ne'er shall drift apart.
> Amidst the colors, hues so bright,
> A clue awaits, hidden from sight.
> In brushstrokes bold, the path unveils,
> A hidden chamber where love prevails.
> Seek the gaze of eyes entwined,
> To the hidden room, you shall find."

"But where is there a hidden room?" Genevieve demanded.

Ashford picked up the picture and replaced it on the wall. "What are all four of them looking at?"

"The sky."

"No, the one room in the house with a light in the window. In the attic, the room must be in the north wing that extends from the house." He stepped back from the painting. "Over the library. But we must hurry."

They rushed out into the back hall. Genevieve started to go back the way they came. "No. Not that way. Going through the billiard room to the staircase will be faster. There won't be anyone there. Westerfield closes the room during the ball."

They hurried through the gallery and slipped quietly into the billiard room.

"Genevieve."

She came to a halt, her heart beating furiously. She turned and came face-to-face with her mother.

"Alone. With him." Lady Grenfell gave him a searing glare and then turned to her daughter. "Your absence has been noticed by many people. What would you have me tell them? That you are alone with a man, with this, this rake. And one of the worst kind. He is handsome to look at and has a quick wit. He may even have a title, but it is an empty one. He's penniless and lives off Westerfield. He has nothing to offer you. I shall not allow it.

"I told you that by this evening you were to have a suitor. A match has been found and will be announced at midnight."

Before she could utter a word, her mother continued with an air of finality, leaving no room for argument. "You will go directly into the ballroom. We shall see if I can preserve the family's reputation."

Her resolve was wavering, and Genevieve reluctantly complied with her mother's demand. As they stepped into the grand hall, she glanced at Ashford, her eyes conveying disappointment and yearning. She knew they had to abide by the rules, but the spark of adventure and connection they had discovered together was slipping away.

Ashford trailed behind, lingering at the entrance to the ballroom.

Lady Grenfell, still not satisfied, turned her attention to Ashford. "And you," she spoke firmly, "will not enter the ballroom with Genevieve and give the impression that the two of you have been at anything. You have put Genevieve in great jeopardy. What will people think?"

"I assure you, Lady Grenfell, there was no intention to cause any harm," he replied, his voice respectful despite his frustration. "I hold Genevieve in the highest regard and would never wish to jeopardize her reputation or happiness. I shall respect your wishes and keep my distance."

From the other side of the ballroom, Ashford watched as Lady Grenfell and Genevieve spoke with people. Genevieve stood with her back to the wall, looking across the ballroom floor. Her eyes never left his.

"There you are, Ashford. Come with me." Westerfield beckoned him. "The music will begin again, and she will want to dance."

"I will not jeopardize her," Ashford said to his uncle as he followed him. Still, his eyes remained fixed on Genevieve as a gentleman approached her. He assumed to ask her to dance. This was torture. He needed to know what she wanted to do, but it was up to Genevieve. All he could do was wait.

As the music started, he took a glass of wine to quell the tension that turned his stomach into a knot.

"I'd like to dance." Genevieve's voice reached him. He turned to see her standing there.

Without hesitation, Genevieve took Ashford's arm, her eyes filled with affection. "With you. No one else. Ever."

Her mother glanced at them, then at Westerfield. Genevieve gave her mother a sympathetic look, silently asking her to understand. Her mother finally gave them a slight nod.

The tension eased, and Ashford escorted her into the center of the ballroom underneath the large Venetian glass chandelier. The candles were placed in a manner that the candlelight created a pattern in all sorts of colors.

As they danced past Westerfield, he said, "You haven't much time. Hurry. I'll detain Lady Grenfell."

Genevieve and Ashford glanced at her mother, then danced their way to the main staircase and hurried to the attic.

Chapter Six

Ashford and Genevieve reached the third floor, where he guided her toward the attic. In a dimly lit alcove beside the attic door, Ashford swiftly chose a lantern, its brass frame shining from the corridor's dim light. With practiced skill, he lit the candle, casting flickering shadows on the walls.

"I'll lead the way," he assured Genevieve. He raised the lantern as they ascended the stairs and arrived at the attic landing.

From the garden, one would assume that the attic rooms were as cozy and well-maintained as the rest of the house. It was all an illusion. As Ashford and Genevieve ventured farther into the attic, he raised the lantern. They noticed that the curtains, the only adornment, were old and tattered. They swung around in the large common room, the light flashing on its contents. Old paintings, furniture, and abandoned trunks rested in a state of disarray and confusion in the center of the room.

With Genevieve at his side, Ashford walked along the wall facing the garden. "How strange. The room we saw in the painting does not appear to exist here. The library extends from the house, and between these two windows, there should be a door leading to the room above the library, the one we saw in the picture."

As he stood at the window, he glanced down at the garden, searching for the spot where the people in the painting had been positioned. He glanced to his left, and to his surprise, he found himself looking into an attic window.

He quickly stepped back from the window, then turned to examine the solid wall. Once again, he peered out at the mysterious window. There had to be some way to access the room. He walked along the wall, tapping it soundly.

"What are you doing?" Genevieve followed with the lantern as he went along.

Ashford stopped and brought her back to the window he had looked out. "What do you see?"

Genevieve looked out, then back at him. "A window."

"To what room?"

She stared at him, unable to give him an answer.

"Exactly." He continued to tap on the wall. "How do you get into that room in this wing of the house? There is no hallway or door."

Intrigued, they followed the wall until they came to a servant's staircase that led to the floor below.

Genevieve ran her hand gently along the wainscoting until she felt something peculiar.

"Here." Ashford was at her side, looking on with interest.

He, too, felt the mechanism and pressed it. They stood staring at each other. A small door had opened.

"I'll go in and have a look," Ashford said. "You stay here."

Genevieve hurried toward the door. "Not without me."

"I don't know what we'll find in there." The glare in her eyes told him there was no way he could win that argument. "Please, I ask that you let me lead this expedition. I do not want to face Lady Grenfell and explain how a ghost or, worse, a goblin did you in." He tried to be serious, but he could not hide his smile.

Genevieve burst out laughing. "Does she unnerve you that much?"

A faint smile touched Ashford's lips. "Not at all. But I could never live with myself if something happened to you, especially if I was accountable for your safety."

Her heart took a sudden dip, then soared back to her chest, reassured by his words. No, he would never allow harm to befall her. "Your protectiveness remains as evident now as it was when we first crossed paths. It's not about being domineering or overbearing, but rather maintaining a calm and non-intimidating manner."

"I would never put you in the jeopardy of facing my mother. You best lead the way. But be aware. I may never give you this boon again."

Carefully, he stepped into the room, looked around, then extended his hand to her. She entered and stood at his side.

Layers of dust blanketed everything in the room. The wallpaper was faded and peeling. The room was sparsely furnished with a bed, a chest, a night table, a writing desk, and two chairs. The atmosphere was tinged with nostalgia and mystery, untouched for what appeared to be a century. Among the dust-covered relics and artifacts, they uncovered several remarkable and sentimental items. Each one was a piece of the puzzle that told the story of Camille and Loren's love and reinforced the timeless nature of their romance.

"This room isn't closed. It's waiting for someone to return." She ventured to the bed. "The bed's been made." She moved over to the chest and found a woman's brush and comb with hair ribbons neatly arranged next to them.

"A servant's room?" he asked as he rummaged through an antique writing desk.

"Not without a door. No. This is a secret room." Genevieve moved on to the shelf. "The items here paint a picture of who they were. There are a few books, a woman's fan, a filled-in dance card, and a bible.

"There are bundles of letters here." Ashford held up one, tied in a faded ribbon that had lost its pink hue years ago. He opened several. "Some are from Camille, while others are from Loren. This must be where they kept their mementos so no one would find them."

She put down the bible and took the letters he handed to her.

He watched her expression become tender, almost embarrassed as she read. "This speaks of stolen moments, secret rendezvous, and an unyielding devotion to one another." She put the letter down. "I do not doubt that they loved each other deeply." She wiped her eyes. "I cannot help but weep for them. What could have been so horrid as to keep them apart?"

"There could be any number of things that may seem unimportant to us, but for them, in their time, were insurmountable. Come, dry your eyes. You had a book in your hand before. What did you find?"

"I found a bible on the shelf." She picked up the book and found several loose pages. "I think this is a journal entry." Genevieve looked at several more pages. "It's a letter." She went back to the beginning.

"Dear Friend,
If you have found this, then you must be very special indeed. I have taken care and remained quiet all these years, but the story burns in my heart. I need to tell someone. So, dear friend, it is you. What I have to tell you is a lesson that

took a long time for me to learn, and once I learned it, I could not put it into practice. You see, it was too late. This is not the rambling of an old woman, but a lesson for you to take to heart.

I remain,

Lady Camille Linwood Hastings, the Duchess of Lost Dreams, written this day, 24th of December 1768."

Genevieve glanced at Ashford. He knew her question. All he did was nod. She began to read to him.

"This is the story of Loren Worthington and Camille Linwood, who were deeply entwined in a passionate and forbidden love affair. Their love story is filled with immense joy and heartache. Their fate was both tragic and hopeful.

"Linwood? That name is familiar to me." Genevieve lowered the letter. "My great-great-grandmother's name was Catherine Linwood." She raised the paper and continued to read.

"Loren Worthington, the charming and enigmatic rake, was the second son of a powerful Duke, destined to inherit a substantial income without the burden of managing an estate. With his brother's marriage providing him with five sons, he had no hope of inheriting.

"Camille Linwood, on the other hand, was the spirited and independent daughter of the Duc of Mayotte, whose mother demanded nothing less than a wealthy well-situated English duke for her daughter. A love match would be a coincidence. Her mother studied and schemed as she arranged who Camille would marry.

"Camille and Loren's love blossomed secretly, finding solace and stolen moments in hidden corners of his sister's home, Westerfield House. Mary and Thomas were a love match and an inspiration to them both.

Westerfield House was where they met on Christmas Eve of 1710. Over the years, they exchanged passionate letters and vows of eternal devotion. A brooch Loren gave Camille became a symbol of their love, containing a cherished acrostic message of their affection for each other."

Genevieve stopped. Her heart pounded at the mention of the Christmas brooch.

Ashford took the papers from her and continued to read.

"As their love story continued to unfold, it became increasingly difficult for them to hide their feelings. One day as they strolled around the lake, Camille's disapproving mother came upon them.

"Pressured to conform, Camille was torn between her love for Loren and the expectations placed upon her. In desperation and with a great deal of heartache, they made the painful decision to part ways, sacrificing their happiness to follow society's demands.

"Loren, heartbroken, chose to travel abroad, seeking relief in distant lands and attempting to mend his broken heart.

"Camille struggled whether to follow her heart and her duty, was married off to a suitable suitor on the 24th of December 1716, a marriage of convenience that stifled her spirit and left her yearning for the love she had lost.

"For years, Camille and Loren lived separate lives, each haunted by the memory of their lost love. Loren wandered the world, seeking adventure and solace. At the same time, Camille carried the weight of duty and the burden of a loveless marriage.

"Despite the passing of time, the Christmas brooch, once a symbol of their passionate love, remained a treasured keepsake for both of them. It held the essence of their connection, a silent testament to a love that defied the constraints of society.

"One fateful Christmas Eve, years later, Loren returned to Westerfield House, his heart still aching for the woman he had never stopped loving. Camille, too, found herself at the house, a widow.

"Destiny played its hand that night as they crossed paths in the grand halls of the house once more. The years melted away, and the spark that had ignited their hearts so long ago reignited with an intensity that could not be denied.

"With the Christmas brooch as a symbol of their timeless love, they made a solemn pact to be together, no matter the consequences. Society's rules and expectations no longer held power over them. Their passion had transcended time. They were determined to create their own destiny.

"Hand in hand, they faced the disapproval and judgment of those who once sought to keep them apart. With the strength of their love and the courage of their hearts, they defied the odds and chose each other, reclaiming the love that had been stolen from them years before.

"And so, the Christmas brooch became a beacon of hope and love, guiding them on a path of passion and devotion. Once lost in the shadows, their love story was now celebrated and cherished, a testament to the enduring power of true love.

"As the clock struck midnight on that magical Christmas Eve, they danced under the shimmering stars, surrounded by the echoes of past love and the promise of a future filled with joy and happiness.

"And in the warmth of each other's arms, they finally found the home they had been searching for all along.

"I will speak for them both. It isn't about the time they lost, but about the time they had together. That will always be cherished and celebrated. But the ton did nothing for either of them. They gossiped and wagged their tongues until some other poor soul fell from grace and became their tasty tidbit.

"Perhaps my destiny is to tell you Camille and Loren's story, my story, so you don't fall prey to the ton but rather find your happy ever after. The happy ever after you deserve.

"The final test is near as you dance under the blush of Christmas and decide which path you take. Do you deny your happiness or revel in your love? Find the Christmas brooch. Find your destiny."

Ashford paged through the Bible and came across a sheet of paper. With care, he removed the document and gently unfolded it. "It's a family tree."

"It could very well be the one that Westerfield mentioned was missing from the library," Genevieve's gaze was fixed on the document. "Who would put it with these papers?"

Ashford placed the paper on the desk. "I surmise that it's a deliberate attempt to either safeguard or hide important lineage information."

Genevieve came alongside him, scanning the document for familiar names and connections.

"Here, it notes the wedding of Thomas Talbot and Mary Worthington."

"Wasn't Mary Loren's sister?" Genevieve asked, still focused on the details in the document.

"Indeed." Ashford's attention shifted to the pages in the back of the Bible. "Families often used their Bibles to maintain records of births and marriages."

"But there are so many pages to sift through. I'm certain it is almost midnight."

A soft smile tugged at the corners of Ashford's mouth. "You're right. Perhaps we should continue our investigation with fresh eyes tomorrow."

"We can't do that. Westerfield said the challenge must be completed before the last stroke of midnight. You don't expect us to give up now?"

"Of course not. We have the date." He turned the page to 1688, looked down the list, and handed the Bible to Genevieve.

"Thomas John Talbot and Mary Helen Worthington married on the 25th of December 1688. The wedding was witnessed by Loren Worthington, the bride's brother, and Celeste Talbot, the groom's sister. The bride's cousin, Richard de Caulet, the Duc of Mayotte, took the place of the bride's recently deceased father, Cecile Worthington, Duke of Whitaker."

She lowered the Bible and stared at him.

"What is it?" Ashford asked.

"Richard de Caulet was my mother's great-grandfather and Catherine's husband." She took up the book. "This means Camille Linwood and I are related." She looked at Ashford. "As you are related to Loren Worthington."

Genevieve put down the book and studied the family tree. "I do not see Loren or Camille."

Ashford stroked the Bible's old leather binding. "In everything we've read and seen, Camille and Loren's love has been constant."

"Were they prevented from being together and forced to sacrifice their love?" Genevieve gazed into Ashford's eyes. "It sounds so much like our story. Don't we deserve to create our own future, the future we want?" She looked toward the small door. "We must find the brooch."

"Do you think there is magic in the Christmas brooch?" Ashford asked as he held her close.

"I want to believe there is." She looked at him and tried to smile. Would their story end the same way as Loren and Camille's? "We took on a challenge, and the end is so close. I'm not going to give up."

"And you want to know your destiny. I do as well. We haven't much time."

Genevieve stepped out of his embrace and picked up Camille's story.

"I think Camille told us where to look next." She eagerly went through the pages, "Here it is." She showed him a page, pointing to a specific sentence.

"The final test is near as you dance under the blush of Christmas and decide which path you take. Do you deny your happiness or revel in your love? Find the Christmas brooch. Find your destiny.

"What should we do?"

"Genevieve." She looked up and studied Ashton's face. "You are the one who has the greatest to lose," he said, "You are the one who must make this decision."

"Aren't we both impacted by what we decide?"

"I have made my decision. I made it when I saw you in the library. With all my heart, I hoped it was you who stood at the bookshelf, and I was not disappointed. You are correct. Like Camille and Loren, our lives will change one way or another."

She put her finger against his lips, silencing him.

"I am aware that my decision may significantly impact others, particularly my mother." Genevieve's eyes grew misty as her lips curled into a tender smile. She looked at Ashford, hoping he would understand her mother without her needing to voice it.

"She is not an evil person. We need to remind her that love doesn't see the boundaries of the *ton* and that not everyone fits into the rules demanded by others. Sometimes, rules must be broken."

Genevieve, her hands gently on his cheeks, drew him closer and kissed him. "I love you. I do not want to spend my life as I have the last five years dreaming of you and looking for you in a crowd, settling for someone my mother has chosen. I want you."

He kissed her thoroughly as a clock struck a quarter to midnight.

"We must go where Camille sent us—to the ballroom. Where else would we dance?" She took the Bible with her.

Chapter Seven

Genevieve and Ashford hurried into the ballroom and found it was empty.

"Everyone is on the terrace, waiting for the fireworks to begin." Ashford scanned the room. "I don't see anywhere to look."

Genevieve took out the papers and read aloud. "*The final test is near as you dance under the blush of Christmas.*"

"There is barely anything here that indicates Christmas." He looked overhead. "Except for the chandelier. A garland of holly and sprigs of mistletoe is the only adornment that…"

He quickly focused on Genevieve. She, too, was staring at the chandelier.

"The blush of Christmas. A kiss under the mistletoe. The brooch must be hidden amidst the chandelier."

"I've been looking for you." Westerfield entered the ballroom. "It's nearly midnight. Have you found the Christmas brooch?"

Genevieve and Ashford looked up at the chandelier. "Not in our hands."

Westerfield followed their gaze and then back at them. "Benson," he called, "a ladder."

"It might be hidden in the chandelier's crown or on the column. It would be difficult to find the brooch among all the colored crystals." Genevieve nervously stood by while the ladder was put in place.

"What is the brooch's secret?" Westerfield and Benson held the ladder while Ashford climbed higher.

"We don't think there is anything magical about the brooch. It's a symbol, a reminder."

"We didn't learn anything we didn't already know," Genevieve told Westerfield. "There shall always be obstacles, but we must embrace forgiveness and believe in second chances. That is the power of love. We found Camille and Loren's great love story."

Her eyes met Ashford's, and he nodded. "As well as one for our future. Our story began with Ashford's determination to help and protect me. And I was just as determined to support him. All these years, we thought of each other and denied anyone else our hearts. We may have met too soon, but we experienced a sampling of the love in store."

Ashford looked down at them. "I saw her emerald eyes everywhere."

"And I saw his rakish mischievous smile that melted my heart."

Curiosity got the better of Westerfield. "Be careful. What are you doing?" he asked, concerned as Ashford leaned into the chandelier, making it sway gently. He pulled his hand away, holding the gem.

"I can't believe it." Westerfield turned toward her. "You've found it."

The clock began to strike the hour as Ashford came down the ladder and placed the brooch in Genevieve's hand.

"The brooch went unnoticed among all the color crystals."

"It's exquisite," Genevieve said as Ashford turned the pin over, the clock sounding the second strike of the hour. "But where is our destiny? I do not see any message."

"It's right in front of you." Westerfield extended his hand toward the gem as the clock sounded the third strike of the hour. "Look carefully at the stones. Can you identify them?"

The clock sounded the fourth strike of the hour.

"The stone in the middle is a diamond." Ashford offered.

"The stones around the diamond are a garnet, lapis, and an amethyst." Genevieve stared at His Grace, silently asking him for their meaning. The clock sounded the fifth strike of the hour.

"The garnet signifies fire and passion. It's for Camille," the duke said. He turned to Genevieve. "That is your middle name, is it not?"

She nodded—an acrostic message.

"The lapis, truth, and wisdom must be for Loren," she said as the clock sounded the sixth strike of the hour.

"That is my middle name."

Genevieve spun around and faced Ashford. "You didn't say anything before."

His Grace nodded. "The diamond is for everlasting love, and the amethyst is—"

"For protection," Ashford added.

As the clock continued to strike midnight, Ashford took a deep breath and looked into Genevieve's eyes. "Genevieve, let us learn from Camille and Loren. It is you I have loved. Marry me." The clock sounded the eighth strike of the hour.

"Genevieve. I forbid you to marry this man," her mother bellowed.

Westerfield stared at her parents as they entered the room, and the clock continued on.

But Genevieve's gaze remained steadfastly fixed on Ashford as she replied, "Yes, I will marry you."

"Genevieve, are you willing to give up everything for him?" her mother pressed.

Still looking into Ashford's eyes, she answered with conviction, "I have dreamt of him for five years. I have said no to every suitor. No one can compare to him. Yes, I would give up everything to be with him." Genevieve turned and faced her mother. "Just as you did for Father when you found the brooch and learned to follow your heart."

Lady Grenfell, stunned by the revelation, stood still with her hand at her throat. "How do you know?"

Genevieve calmly handed her mother the Bible. "It's all there. Written in your handwriting. Along with the family tree. You were at the Christmas ball."

"Yes. It is my handwriting." Her mother didn't have to look at the pages. "Lady Camille was ill and unable to write. She asked me to pen the words for her. Afterward, she brought me to the secret attic room, where I found the brooch. After the ball"—she turned to Westerfield— "you hid the brooch in the chandelier."

The fireworks began to go off, casting different hues across the ballroom.

"You followed your destiny," Genevieve asked. "Why would you want anything less for me?"

"But I didn't. My destiny was with someone else." Her mother's fleeting glance at Westerfield told Genevieve all she needed to know.

"Your mother and I interpreted our destinies differently. Although she insisted I didn't accept my destiny," Westerfield offered. "I was worse than a rogue. I was selfish and even more arrogant than I am today if you can imagine that." He let out a nervous laugh.

"My destiny was elsewhere. Years later, when your mother met Grenfell, she knew I had been correct." Westerfield let out a deep sigh. "Perhaps that is why she didn't want you to look for your destiny in the ramblings of an old woman or the acrostic code of a brooch—"

"But in your heart," her mother gently interjected, a knowing smile on her lips, "not in a prescribed story, and not even in tradition. The brooch told me that I would find love and happiness in the future." Her mother looked at Westerfield.

"Love is not the answer for everyone. The brooch told me my destiny would be in business."

Genevieve hadn't left Ashford's side, her heart swelling with the weight of their shared journey. "We discovered so much more today than the musings of an old woman or the hidden message in the brooch." Genevieve turned to Ashford, a tender smile on her lips. "Both our lives changed the day Ashford came to my rescue. I was destined to be with him and no one else. We've remained loyal to one another, patiently waiting for the day we'd be reunited."

Westerfield's prideful gaze bore into Ashford. "There is no man more suitable for Genevieve than Ashford. Grenfell and I have had the privilege of working alongside him for the last three years. Not only is he a suitable partner for Genevieve, he also expanded both our estates and his own, as well as achieving notable successes, earning the respect of those around him."

Genevieve's father stepped beside her mother. His voice was full of understanding and approval. "My dear, I understand your apprehension and your concern about convention. Yet, if there's anyone who can influence the *ton* and reshape their perspective on a situation, it's you. No one else possesses your strength and insight."

Ashford's hand found Genevieve's, their fingers intertwining like the threads of destiny itself. A promise of a lifetime's worth of shared experiences and unspoken promises passed between them. "I vow to cherish and protect Genevieve for all my days," he declared, his voice unwavering and sincere.

Genevieve's eyes glistened. "And I promise to stand by your side through every challenge and triumph that comes our way."

As the Christmas fireworks that glittered in the night sky came to an end, the ballroom doors swung open. Still captivated by the breathtaking display, the guests streamed in. Genevieve and Ashford stood at the heart of the ballroom, their hands still intertwined.

Amidst the anticipation, Lord Westerfield stepped forward, commanding everyone's attention. His voice, a rich timbre that resonated with authority, carried throughout the room. "Ladies and gentlemen." His eyes twinkled with a secret delight. "Tonight, after one hundred years of searching, the long-lost treasure has been found."

Gasps of surprise and curiosity rippled through the crowd. Westerfield's gaze turned to Genevieve and Ashford. "I am pleased to announce that Lady Genevieve and Lord Ashford have uncovered the elusive Christmas brooch—a symbol of history, mystery, and the enduring power of love."

In the glow of the ballroom, everyone celebrated the end of the grand adventure. As the applause faded, Genevieve turned to Ashford. "We did it," she whispered, her voice trembling.

He smiled, his thumb brushing gently over the back of her hand. "Yes, we did. Finding our destiny was the goal, but the treasure we've found is so much more."

She leaned in, their foreheads touching in a moment of quiet intimacy. "Our destiny wasn't to *find* love. It was to uncover the strength and resilience of our love for one another."

Ashford's voice held a promise as he whispered back, "Just as the Christmas brooch holds hidden messages, our story proves that true love shines brightest for those who look deeper."

His gaze shifted upward at a sprig of mistletoe.

Following his gaze, she saw the mistletoe.

He drew her into his arms. "All my love is yours."

Genevieve held him tightly. "As mine is yours."

He leaned in, his lips gently meeting hers in a tender kiss, promising a future full of love and devotion. With open hearts, they embraced the path that destiny had laid before them, ready to confront any trials and revel in every moment of joy that awaited them.

The End

♥ ♥ ♥

I hope you enjoyed reading "The Lady and the Christmas Brooch" and that it brought a touch of historical magic to your holiday season!

Your thoughts mean the world to me. If you have a moment, I'd love it if you could share your review on the site where you purchased your copy, or on a reader site such as Goodreads. Your feedback helps me craft more enchanting tales for you to enjoy.

To stay updated on new releases, appearances, and more exciting news, consider subscribing to my newsletter. As a special thank you, you'll receive a free book as a gift! Newsletter

Happy reading, and may your days be filled with romance and adventure.

P.S. As a little treat, here's a sneak peek into the first chapter of The Lady and the Barrister. I hope you find the glimpse as tantalizing as found writing it. Enjoy.

Warmly,
Ruth

♥ ♥ ♥

The Lady and the Barrister

She swore she'd help him find his soul mate.
Will she realize he has met his match?

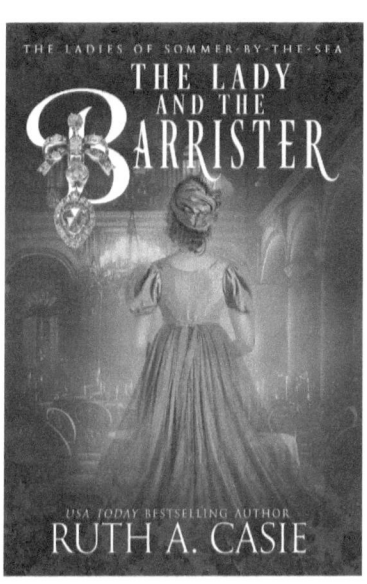

Lady Anna Ravencroft shines brightly as a much-admired organizer and hostess. In her mind it is the one thing at which she succeeds. Inwardly she is shy, retiring… a wallflower. With two failed seasons that ended in disaster she has accepted marriage might not be in her future.

Lord Fraser Castleton, a London barrister is shocked when he inherits a title and estate from his mother's great aunt and becomes the 8th Duke of Willbury. He returns to Sommer-by-the-Sea to take up permanent residence. He crosses paths with his longtime friend, Lady Anna. He confides that he is the target of every mother with an unmarried daughter. She commiserates with him. Every eligible gentleman sees the Ravencroft purse rather than her. Together they decide to find a mate for each other. Anna presents him with a list of several eligible women. Castleton is receptive, but not enthusiastic. He gives her the same reaction with the subsequent two lists. Will she realize he has already found his match?

Reginald Younge, who doesn't always play by the rules, wants to be the next Member of Parliament for his borough. His political backer will support him if Younge can finance the campaign himself. He suggests Younge find a wealthy wife to support his political plans. Marrying a Ravencroft would all but guarantee not only his backer's continued support but provide the steady stream of money needed to claim his place amongst the gentry. He calls on Lady Anna for assistance with a campaign event and has an ulterior motive.

The Lady and the Barrister ~ Excerpt
Book One – The Return of the Ladies of Sommer-by-the-Sea

Prologue

The last time Lady Marianna Ravencroft sat with Captain Fraser Castleton, Retd, for any length of time, was the summer of 1809, five years ago when he joined her for tea. They sat in her garden at Raven Hall and talked for hours.

Well, he talked. She listened. They knew each other growing up and enjoyed each other's company. It didn't take long before they once again teased each other, sliding back into that comfortable place.

Anna, a soft smile on her lips, couldn't keep from looking at him. Not to stare, but to make sure he was really there. His natural open presence was welcoming. There was still a hint of his wild warrior ways. Life's design had taught him to harness that energy to transform him into a secure, confident, compassionate man. He was ruggedly handsome. Perhaps that was the lasting effect of his wild days. She chuckled to herself.

She took a deeper look and relented. He was physically handsome with his dark wavy hair just a bit too long, his well-trimmed beard, his blue green eyes just a bit too bright, and a devastating smile that always curled her toes. She let out a breath and tried to relax said toes.

Their time together was more than pleasant, although she did notice there was one part of his life he would not divulge. He skirted around the horrors he experienced during his five years in the service until finally he seemed to run out of words. The only ones left were about the war. About his brother, Lucian.

The silence went on for several agonizing minutes. Mrs. Cutler, Ravencroft's housekeeper, brought a plate of tarts and ginger biscuits along with a pot of tea. Still, he said nothing. Anna poured his tea and fortified it with a splash of her father's brandy. His chest heaved, and he let the air out slowly. His face turned into a mask of pain, hurt, anger, and acceptance all rolled into one.

"I've buried Lucian's death deep. Every time I think I can talk about it…" He stared at his shaking hands then at her.

"When you want to talk, I'm here to listen." Anna covered his hands with her own, a surprising warmth spread through her.

His breathing was ragged as he struggled for control.

"You have no idea. Imagine the worst thing you can think of. That is not half as bad as what I observed." He paused. "What I had to do. Things I want to tell you but cannot." His voice was barely a whisper.

Oh, but she did have some insight. He wasn't aware that she and her friend Lady Harriet Manning had helped soldiers who returned from the war. Hattie was a beautiful person inside and out. On the outside, she had a trim frame, fine features, and expressive amber eyes. Her hair, when not neatly gathered in a knot at the base of her neck, was long and thick. It was the most interesting shade of a reddish brown, the color of fine burgundy.

On the inside, Hattie was a compassionate caregiver. Medically trained by her father, the Earl of Manning and a renowned physician, Hattie in turn taught Anna what to do. Together, they nursed men physically and mentally. Each man was a survivor, a hero, not a victim of Napoleon and his war.

For now, she remained quiet. Castleton needed to talk.

"The brutality. What one man is capable of doing to another. A man you never met. A man just as scared as you." Castleton said nothing for a few minutes. "That was four years ago, and to me, it was yesterday."

What went on in his head? From his grimace, she suspected he continued to fight an internal battle. She wanted to put her arms around him and give him her strength, but that would do more harm than good. Instead, she waited and listened.

"Lucian and I served together. We were never far from each other. Barrington sent us to assist Vice-Admiral Nelson." He closed his eyes.

Anna schooled herself not to react, but dear God, he was back in the thick of it all, on the *HMS Victory*.

"Captain Hardy, Lucian, and I were on Victory's deck with the Vice-Admiral as he paced the quarterdeck with the battle waging around us. A multitude of ordnance exploded in quick succession, creating an echo so painful it felt as if your head was about to burst.

"With each explosion came the sound of splintering wood, the crash of debris into the water or onto the deck. But worse were the screams and groans of the wounded men. We strained to hear our orders over the din."

Anna sat numb. For her, he painted vivid, terrible pictures. They were more horrendous for Castleton. Now, months later, he was back in the middle of it, seeing the explosions, smelling the gunpowder, and hearing the screams. Reliving it again, as if once wasn't enough.

"In the tumult, no one heard the blast of a single rifle, but a single shot it was. Fired from the mizzen of the French ship *Redoubtable*. The shot hit Nelson in his left shoulder. He collapsed at my feet. I went to his aid, but he wouldn't let me carry him. Instead, I helped him to his feet and gave him my shoulder.

"Before I went below deck, I saw Lucian run to the gunwale with his rifle raised. He got his shot off. The assassin did as well. I watched the man fall from the mizzen. Hardy urged me to take Nelson below. I didn't know the assassin's shot had been true, that he shot Lucian in his chest."

The pain in his eyes tore at her, but she couldn't do or say anything to comfort him. *Let him talk.*

"While I helped Nelson, my brother, my twin brother lay dying above me." He stared into the garden. "I didn't sit with him. Help him. Ease his way. I didn't... say good-bye." His words trailed off. Silent for several minutes, at last he took a deep breath. "When I found him, I cradled him in my arms, and I vowed with all my heart that I would finish his mission and care for those he held dear." He stared at her with watery eyes. "And cried."

Anna couldn't sit still a moment longer. She knelt next to his chair, put her arm around him, and held him close.

They sat without speaking, her throat knotted and hot with grief. She couldn't say anything if she wanted to. And if she did speak, what would she say? She was sorry for his loss? She understood how he felt? All empty words that held little meaning and meant less.

Anna gently placed her hand over his.

Castleton turned over his hand and intertwined his fingers with hers. After what seemed like hours, he gazed at her. Raw hurt glittered in his eyes. He gently squeezed her hand before he released her.

She went back to her seat.

"What will you do now?" She might as well finish what she started even though his answer was not what she wanted to hear. She removed the last tart from the serving dish and put it on his plate.

Mrs. Cutler brought in a fresh pot of tea and heated Castleton's cup.

"Thank you, Mrs. Cutler." One corner of his mouth pulled into a smile. "I missed your tarts."

"At least now you're not pilfering them and running from my kitchen. I'm too old to run after you with my rolling pin." The housekeeper shook her head.

There was a faint gleam of humor in his eyes, and his mouth curved into an unconscious smile. Anna found his smile catching.

"You're a wonderful and generous woman." Castleton's sincerity took the woman by surprise.

"It was all a hoax. I can tell you now. I made extra tarts for you and your friends."

"But you waved your rolling pin—" His voice rose in feigned surprise.

"And laughed as you grabbed the tarts and ran away. My own lads did the same. I remember the day one of the boys from the village pushed your brother, and he dropped his prize into the pond. You gave him yours and metered out justice, making the unruly boys work off their debt. It was no surprise to me that you became a barrister."

"Ah, that was why a lone tart remained on the cooling rack when I came by the kitchen. You nodded toward the tart and turned your back." A faraway, amused look filled his eyes as he licked his lips.

"I think that was the most delicious tart I ever ate."

"I wouldn't let you go hungry." Mrs. Cutler nodded and withdrew. The misty look on the woman's face caught Anna by surprise.

"I understand now. You're here for Mrs. Cutler's tarts." Anna teased him as she did when they were younger.

"I missed you too, Anna. Unfortunately, I won't be here long. I return to London in the morning. I've decided I must pick up where I left off at the Inns of Court."

She settled back in her chair, disappointed.

"We must write, and you have to plan to visit when you're in London."

"If you are leaving so soon, then I had best give you your present." Anna nodded to the footman who stood by the door.

"Present? What for?" There may have been a trace of denial in his voice, but the childlike expectation of a gift lit up his face.

A furry brown and black ball with a splash of white snorted and happily bounded toward her. The pup made a stop at Castleton's feet, then sat at attention, her eyes bright and her tongue out.

"Fraser Castleton, let me introduce you to Kaiah. She's from a unique breed of herding dogs. She can keep you company on your walks, even in London. You will be the talk of Hyde Park."

Kaiah nuzzled his hand.

"I've tried to teach her proper manners, but she shamelessly craves attention."

He ruffled Kaiah's silky coat.

"Does she play fetch?" He was still stroking her coat.

Anna nodded to Kaiah. The dog trotted off to the garden and brought back a stick. She sat in front of Castleton, put down the toy, and eagerly waited.

They spent the next several minutes with the pup racing in the garden.

Castleton's smile set her at ease. If only she could make him smile that way.

"I've decided to devote myself to my profession." He kept tossing a stick for Kaiah to retrieve.

"That's an admirable goal."

"Aunt Adelaide would have me believe that a well-established profession is followed by a well-established family. I hate to disappoint her, but I see no family in my future."

"No family?" Everyone wanted a family. Family was loving and supporting one another. She couldn't imagine life without her family, and she looked forward to having one of her own. Where was the man who moments ago teased, challenged, and laughed? She had always known there was something special about him, something special between them.

"Every one of us dies. I will never put anyone I love through that hell." There was a finality in his words, in his stance, in his face. He silently pleaded with her to understand.

She didn't have an answer for him.

He stood in the garden playing with Kaiah, but to Anna, he was already gone, and there was nothing she could do to change his mind or bring him back.

He and Kaiah departed the next day. He did come back to Sommer-by-the-Sea to see his Aunt Adelaide, the Duchess of Willbury every so often, but their paths went in different directions.--

♥ ♥ ♥

She swore she'd help him find his soul mate.
Will she realize he has met his match?
Available at <u>Amazon KU</u>

About Ruth A. Casie

RUTH A. CASIE is a *USA Today bestselling author*. She writes historical adventures from the shores of medieval Scotland to the cobblestone streets of Regency London. Within the pages, you'll discover 'edge-of-your-seat' suspense, mind-boggling drama, and heart-melting emotions featuring strong women and the men who deserve them. She currently has four historical series: *The Druid Knight, The Stelton Legacy, and The Ladies of Sommer-by-the-Sea,* and she participates in two connected worlds, *The Lyon's Den* and *The Pirates of Britannia.* The first book in her series, *Barrington's Brigade,* is scheduled to be released in January 2025.

Ruth lives in New Jersey with her hero, three empty bedrooms, and a growing number of incomplete counted cross-stitch projects. Before she found her voice, she was a speech therapist, client liaison for a corrugated manufacturer, and vice president at a major international bank where she was a product/marketing manager. Still, her favorite job is the one she's doing now—writing romance. Grab your favorite cup of tea, or an ale if you prefer, and join her heroes and heroines as they race across the pages to find their happily ever after. Ruth hopes her stories are your next favorite adventures!

For more information on Ruth,
please join her newsletter or visit her online at
www.RuthACasie.com
Ruth@RuthACasie.com

www.ingramcontent.com/pod-product-compliance
Lightning Source LLC
Chambersburg PA
CBHW020342130626
46549CB00003B/1248